USUAL
MONSTERS

BY TREVOR FIRETOG

Haley screamed, her voice tearing through the calm of the sunset. She was nearly at the tree line now, yanked forcefully by a tall, powerful figure.

Jane dropped her gun.

Isaiah led her niece into the woods, and as the trees swallowed them from sight, Haley gave one last cry for help.

This can't be right. Isaiah is only in my mind.

Jane pressed her fists to her temples, as if she could hold her thoughts together by pure force.

Her headache returned with a fury, gripping her brain with what felt like grits of glass. A high-pitched tone filled her ears. She grew dizzy and her knees gave out. She hit the ground, still trying to watch the forest, but her vision blurred with each heartbeat.

Isaiah can't be real.

There's supposed to be no such thing as monsters.

ACKNOWLEDGMENTS

There are many people whom to thank for helping me beat this novella into shape.

James Chambers, friend, mentor, and one hell of a beta-reader.

David Dodd and David Niall Wilson, for taking this book on.

Phil Firetog, for providing me with such a great cover.

Brian Keene, Dallas Mayr, Frank Raymond Michaels, Kristina Lebo, Patrick Freivald, P.D. Cacek, and Fabian Perez, who have all either read this novella in one of its various stages, or have been kind enough to offer me some wonderful advice and guidance while writing it.

My deepest thanks goes out to Detective Bob Lebo of the Bristol Township Police Department, and Adam Torres of the NYPD, who both did their best with answering my endless questions. Any errors or liberties taken with procedure are entirely my own.

My family, without whom this book wouldn't exist.

And of course Courtney, who only read this novella long after the first draft had been written, but never allowed me to give up on it, and pushed me and encouraged me whenever I hit a wall. Which was often.

DEDICATION

For Courtney,
Who always wanted me to do something with this novella. Well,
here you go.

And for anybody out there who has fought, or is still fighting the
hard battle,
Don't give up.

Whoever fights monsters, should see to it that in the process he does not become a monster.

—Nietzsche

CHAPTER 1

Jane awoke and slid the gun into her mouth like she'd done a hundred times before. She'd developed a taste for gunmetal.

The sensation of bits of glass traced a ragged line through the grooves of her brain.

No different than any other morning.

The ringing stopped, and the headache cleared, as it usually did.

Shoving the Smith & Wesson in her mouth helped calm her brain.

She placed the gun back in her nightstand. The headache returned but only with a dull throb. She rubbed her temples with two fingers, trying to steady her breathing the way her doctor showed her.

Acid gurgled in her stomach, sending a burning line up her throat. Ears ringing, she rolled out of bed, dashed to the bathroom and hurled into the toilet. She made a mental note to thank Dan for leaving the toilet seat up.

Brushing the hair from her face, she spat a few times before flushing. She tore a square of toilet paper off the roll and dabbed the corners of her mouth.

Another usual morning, she thought, her head throbbing, stomach quivering.

She stood and gazed into the mirror.

Something gazed back at her.

Jane went numb.

A monster stood behind her, thin as a rail, pale skin hanging loosely off its bones. Its wispy yellow hair stuck straight up from its head and drifted about, as if under water. Its eyes told a story of pain and anguish.

It reached out to Jane, gnarled fingers flexing, grasping, and opened its mouth as if to say something, but it coughed up a mouthful of steam.

"Hello, Jeremiah." Jane said to the mirror. She pulled her toothbrush from the holder at the edge of the sink and unscrewed the cap of the toothpaste. "Good to see you this morning."

The monster groaned and belched and more steam came out of its mouth and nose.

As the steam wafted past Jane, the monster's breath invaded her senses, stung her nostrils, foul and thick.

The doctor told her there were no monsters. If she saw something that shouldn't exist, it was only her illness acting up. If she felt something or tasted something or smelled something that shouldn't be there, it was simply the receptors in her brain crossing wires.

She turned the faucet on the hottest it could go. Steam filled the bathroom. Jeremiah liked that. Jane let the water run until the steam clung to the mirror and hid the monster from her sight.

Another usual morning with another usual monster.

The savory scent and soft sizzle of bacon roused Jane's hunger. In the beginning of her illness, the headaches, combined with the multitude of medication and pills her doctor pushed, caused frequent vomiting. The sick feeling left her with a trembling stomach and an overwhelming need to gag should there be any mention of food. As time passed, her body began to work around that sick feeling. Now, she could be sick and eat a four-course meal right after without giving it a second thought.

In the kitchen, Dan stood over the stove in his police uniform, flipping an omelet. He held the pan over a plate and slid the omelet onto it.

He noticed Jane and then looked down at the pan.

"Morning," he said.

"Good morning," Jane said, sitting in a chair at the dining room table.

"Haley," Dan called, "come get breakfast!"

He pulled two strips of bacon out of another pan and placed them on the plate next to the eggs.

"You want anything special in your omelet?" he asked,

cracking two more eggs into a dish and stirring them with a fork.

"With cheese is fine."

He slid an empty plate in front of her. "You got it."

Dan gave her a charming wink and proceeded to make her breakfast.

No matter how many times she'd seen him in uniform, she always found him sexy. Perhaps it was in the way the black shirt clung to his biceps, or maybe how he wore the shining badge on his chest, with power and confidence.

She missed that most about being on the force: the confidence the shield gave her. She could use some of that now. She used to say that even if she lived to be one hundred, she'd never leave the force, as long as she still had some juice left in her.

What a load of shit.

I won't live to be one hundred. I won't make it past forty.

Her appetite vanished.

"See any of your friends this morning?" Dan said.

"No."

"Are you sure?"

"Yes, why?"

"Would you tell me if you did?"

Jane hesitated and Dan picked up on it. He shook his head and grumbled something to himself.

Haley dashed into the kitchen wearing a T-shirt and jeans. A purple ribbon—a gift Jane had given her—held back her hair, as it always did. Her book bag, looking several sizes too big for a girl her age, hung over her shoulder. She took a forkful of omelet from the counter.

"Hey, Aunt Jane." She chewed. "The bus is outside."

"Go," Dan said.

"Okay." Haley wouldn't look at him.

She wrapped her arms around Jane, hugged her and gave her a peck on the cheek. "Bye."

"Bye, sweetie."

"Picking you up around three-thirty, okay?" Dan called.

"Can Aunt Jane pick me up?"

"No, and I'm not having this discussion with you again."

"Okay," she whispered softly as she made her way out the door.

The door closed and for a moment Jane and Dan held their breaths in the silence.

"I'm sorry I lied about my friends," Jane said.

"It's fine." Dan slid the omelet she no longer wanted onto her plate.

"I just didn't want you to think things were getting worse. Because they're not."

"Have you given any more thought to it?"

"I don't know what you're talking about."

"Checking yourself in—"

"I'm *sure* I don't know what you're talking about."

"Hospice—"

"*Hospice* is for people on their way out. *Hospice* is for people who can't care for themselves anymore. Is that what you think of me? Am I a burden to you?"

His eyes widened and he took a step back, baffled, unsure. He looked at the pan in his hands and then at his wristwatch.

"Look, I have to… I'm late."

He threw the pan in the sink and then rinsed his hands.

Jane stood and blocked the exit of the kitchen.

He approached, waiting for her to move.

"Look, I'm sorry. I'm just so—" she shrugged. "Am I at least going to get a kiss goodbye?"

He brushed his lips against hers and then pushed her out of his way.

"Goodbye," he said.

He walked through the living room and out the front door, slamming it behind him, leaving Jane alone in the house. She thought about crying, but decided that would do her no good.

She sat at the table and forced herself to eat her omelet.

If she ate, maybe Dan would love her again. Maybe the monsters would go away.

And he would touch her, like he did before all this shit happened.

Once she tossed the leftover eggs in the garbage and cleaned the dishes, Jane retreated upstairs for a quick shower to clear her head.

Upstairs another monster waited, watching her from the shadowed hallway. Jane stopped and held her breath. Her shoulders locked, and her legs tensed involuntarily, as if ready to run.

Judging from its towering build, it looked to be Isaiah.

Isaiah had never been inside the house before.

Out of the monsters Jane had seen and named, Isaiah never failed to drain the blood from her face, turn her joints to stone, and leave her starving for breath. It stood maybe seven feet high; its body was incredibly built with bulging knots of muscle. A thick pelt of gray hair started at its chest and trailed down to its abdomen, over skin the blue-gray color of moldy bread. Each of its sharp claws had the size and shine of a kitchen knife.

"What are you doing inside the house, Isaiah?" Jane said, straightening her back, controlling her fear.

I'm stronger than this.

The monster opened its mouth, exposing its teeth, demonstrating its authority. Its mouth held only six teeth, but each jutted out about six inches. When Isaiah's jaw stayed closed, the teeth overlapped, three pointing up to its face, and three hanging down past its chin, all of them perpetually stained with blood.

"I'm just going to take a shower. When I come back, I don't want to see you inside the house."

Isaiah tilted its head and blinked.

The other monsters had predictable times and places of when they'd make an appearance. She could always count on Isaiah to be standing outside the house, watching the family through the windows. Over time, Jane developed the habit of closing the blinds, making him one less monster to worry about.

Until now.

I can't be getting worse. I just can't.

Jane puffed up her chest and proceeded into her bedroom, never severing eye contact with Isaiah.

She closed the door and locked it for good measure. The locks would do nothing against the imaginary monster outside the door, but it gave her a sense of comfort.

She backed away from the door and crouched down on the floor, pressed her back against the bed. Isaiah might be standing on the other side of the door, ready to break it down at any moment. But that wouldn't happen, for this was all in her head.

What could this mean for her, for her illness?

Please, don't let it get any worse.

Once Jane felt sure Isaiah would leave her alone, she picked herself up and went through her drawer, absentmindedly picking out some fresh clothes to wear: a navy-blue tank top and black shorts. She left them in a folded pile on top of her dresser.

She went into the bathroom and turned the water to a lukewarm temperature. If it were any hotter, the steam might attract Jeremiah, and while he often seemed harmless, Jane wanted to be by herself.

She squeezed the shampoo into her hand and lathered it through her hair, scrubbing hard. Scrubbing became scratching and squeezing at her scalp, as if the shampoo might seep in and cleanse her tumor-riddled brain.

As if.

She did her best not to think about what might happen in a few months' time and simply live in the moment, but it was hard with the illness slowly killing her. She'd been dying for two years. The estimated survival time for a cancer like this was eighteen months, give or take. Jane's cancer briefly fell into remission a little over a year ago. It stayed in remission for seven months before coming back harder, with rejuvenated fury, ripping through her brain and leaving sharper headaches in its wake. However, even in remission, Jane knew the tumors hadn't shrunk completely. They'd be back. The monsters she saw every day spoiled the hope of it ever fully going away.

Sometimes anything besides sleep required too much energy. Every monster in her life served as a reminder of what little time remained. She would never watch her niece grow up.

Haley's supposed to graduate elementary school this year. Will I even be around for the ceremony? Will I be able to hold her and kiss her and tell her I'm proud of everything she's done?

The poor girl didn't need this. She needed a family.

Jane turned off the water and stepped out of the tub. A bit of steam hung in the still air, but no Jeremiah, nor anyone else.

Good.

She pulled a towel off the rack and as she patted herself dry, she took a moment to admire the woman in the mirror.

At age thirty-eight, she was more in shape than most girls in their twenties. She wasn't perfect; there was some droop, but she still found herself sexy. The skin across her stomach held tight, and free of stretch marks, perhaps the only good thing about never being pregnant.

Her only flaw might have been the bridge of her nose, slightly crooked from when she broke it in the car accident. The cartilage had been imperfectly reset.

So why wouldn't Dan touch her?

What was wrong with her?

She wrapped the towel around herself and walked into her bedroom.

Enoch waited for her in his usual place, on the floor by her husband's nightstand. This monster always sat hunched over and looked at Jane with sad, restless eyes.

Sometimes Enoch motioned for Jane to come over, pointing at the nightstand. On top of the nightstand sat a picture of Jane, Dan, Haley, and Sarah—Jane's sister—taken on a trip to the Bronx zoo. The picture was five years old, before Jane had been diagnosed.

It seemed Enoch liked to remind her of what her life used to be like.

Thanks, Enoch.

Enoch looked up at her, his eyes big and glassy. He hugged the nightstand tighter, on the verge of tears.

"What's wrong?" she said.

Enoch's body was a gaunt mess, so thin he might have been only bones with a sheet of gray paper skin spread across them. His perfectly rounded head showed a pronounced brow and crinkled nose. His eyes were huge and full of wonder and sadness. Pink, pus-swollen lesions covered his hairless body.

The one time Jane had seen Enoch away from the nightstand, the poor thing moved awkwardly, like someone old and in terrible pain.

He was the only monster that Jane felt bad for and wanted to help. He looked worse and worse with every visit.

Enoch tightened his grip around the stand and started to heave. He opened his mouth and screamed, but Jane heard nothing more than a dull moan from something that sounded far away. He did this often. Jane could never understand him.

It must be frustrating, to be trying so hard, but never understood.

Jane pulled her eyes away from Enoch and crawled into bed, not bothering to put on the clothes she'd left out. Fatigue settled into her bones, and even though she'd woken up a couple hours ago, a little nap might do her good. Enoch watched her, peeking over the bed from the other side.

Jane often thought the creature resembled herself. Every time she saw him, he looked worse than before, like he was decaying.

He could have been guarding that picture on the nightstand because he knew it was her last connection to a time when she felt normal, before monsters. The life she used to have, fading before her eyes.

She hoped if Enoch withered away and died, maybe she wouldn't have to.

It wasn't selfish. After all, Enoch was only a figment of her diseased imagination.

Jane closed her eyes and tried not to think about death or monsters or hospice.

Chapter 2

When Jane woke up, she rolled onto her back and started coughing. She tried to sit up, but the pain in her head was too intense.

She scrambled to her nightstand for her gun. With agony-blurred eyes, she unstrapped it from the holster and put it in her mouth. She almost laughed at the situation, holding herself at gunpoint, threatening the pain to go away.

It always worked.

The gun never had a clip in it and hadn't been loaded in the past two years. Part of her knew it would always be safe. But another part of her, a more primal part, reacted to the illusion of danger. The gun provided her with the clarity her headaches had robbed from her.

With her headache diminished, but not quite gone, Jane slowly removed the gun from her mouth, hands still shaking from residual pain, and placed it back on the nightstand. The time on her alarm clock read 6:43 P.M.

The sky through her bedroom window cast the world in dim blue, as the last of the day's sunlight slipped away. She'd slept through the whole day.

Jane threw off the covers and rose out of bed. She went to her dresser to put on her clothes, but the outfit she'd picked out before was no longer there. She opened the drawers and pulled out new clothes, an old police department T-shirt, panties, and jeans.

She had probably missed dinner. No one had tried to wake her up.

They should be home by now, shouldn't they?

A feeling of loneliness hung over the silent house.

She glanced at Dan's nightstand. Enoch wasn't there.

As Jane finished putting on her clothes, she ran her fingers through her sleep-tangled hair and attempted to put on her best *everything-is-okay* smile.

A shrill scream broke the silence of the house, followed by a crash of glass. Jane's knees trembled, and her teeth ground together.

She rushed to her nightstand and grabbed her Smith & Wesson. She opened the top drawer and found the clip with fifteen rounds, tucked safely away in the back.

Jane loaded the gun for the first time since leaving the force.

She racked the slide with a satisfying *click*, chambering her first round.

Another scream.

Jane left her bedroom and stealthily proceeded into the dark hallway. Either the power had gone out, or no one had turned on the lights.

Her heart hammered in her chest, and her headache finally left her alone. She walked quickly, yet carefully, keeping her knees bent, walking on the balls of her feet, ready to break out into a run if need be.

She felt like a cop again.

She went down the stairs, keeping her ears open for any other sounds. In the living room, she saw straight through to her kitchen. The sliding glass door was shattered.

The television flickered with pale images from a show or movie Jane had never seen before. The power wasn't out.

If Jane hadn't looked down at that moment, if the television hadn't cast a cutting, unpleasant light on the ground, she might have not noticed him. She might have stepped on him and not realized.

Dan lay on the floor on his back, still in uniform.

His torso had been split open down the middle, and spread apart. His ribcage had been broken and pulled, so that each bone jutted straight up in the air like long, thin fingers, reaching. Strands of his entrails were spilled out of his stomach and weaved around the floor in wet coils that formed an almost deliberate design.

Jane whimpered a small, but ferocious, cry.

Her husband's face was calm, at peace, as if he might have been sleeping, and that made Jane's pain burn brighter.

She backed away from the body, for that's all he was now: a body. That's how she'd been trained to think in these situations. He was no longer the man who once loved her, who nuzzled her and kissed her.

A sharp cry broke Jane's trance. It came from the back yard.

Jane stepped past her husband's body, creeping toward the shattered glass door.

Careful not to step on the shards with bare feet, she tiptoed outside, where a flash of movement caught her eye.

Her stomach flipped.

Haley screamed, her voice tearing through the calm of the sunset. She was nearly at the tree line now, yanked forcefully by a tall, powerful figure.

Jane dropped her gun.

Isaiah led her niece into the woods, and as the trees swallowed them from sight, Haley gave one last cry for help.

This can't be right. Isaiah is only in my mind.

Jane pressed her fists to her temples, as if she could hold her thoughts together by pure force.

Her headache returned with a fury, gripping her brain with what felt like grits of glass. A high-pitched tone filled her ears. She grew dizzy and her knees gave out. She hit the ground, still trying to watch the forest, but her vision blurred with each heartbeat.

Isaiah can't be real.

There's supposed to be no such thing as monsters.

CHAPTER 3

"Holy hell," Naomi said.

Jane ran the back of her hand under her nose and blinked away the last of her tears. They sat side by side on the porch swing outside the house. Officers and EMTs went in and out of her home, while the familiar red and blue lights from police cars lit the night like silent fireworks.

Naomi had been Jane's best friend, as well as her ex-partner. For only living down the street, Jane thought they weren't in each other's lives nearly as much as they should have been. Naomi was a working girl, still on the force, but recently had been promoted to detective. Sometimes, Jane thought, the only way to be able to talk to her was to dial 911.

"He was a good cop, a good man. Fuck." Naomi hunched over and pushed her head against her knees.

She was off duty tonight and came over simply because she saw the commotion from down the street.

"And we'll find Haley, trust me. We will," Naomi said, lifting her head, "and we'll nab the sonovabitch that did this."

Haley. Being pulled into the woods by... someone.

It was dark, hard to tell.

After Jane had recovered from her faint, she stumbled into the house, broken glass from the door sliced at her feet, but she felt numb to the pain. She grabbed the phone and dialed the police. Immediately recognized the voice of the dispatcher as Officer Zimbric. He, in turn, recognized her voice, sensed her distress, her directionless rambling about monsters killing her husband, and immediately sent out all available units.

He was always so nice to her.

Jane went up to her bedroom, locked the door, and waited

for the police to arrive. While waiting, the clouds in her head disappeared and she finally settled on a story to tell the police, and this story was monster free.

No one questioned Jane's mention of monsters over the phone. For all they knew, Jane meant whoever did this was indeed a monster in the human sense. Hell, she didn't think anyone even knew about her hallucinations.

Could they even be called hallucinations anymore?

Of course they are. There's no proof Isaiah took her. It was dark and I have a condition.

"I'm not going to sugarcoat it. You know as well as I do this doesn't look good. It's just procedure. I can't imagine how hard this must be. But I promise things will get better."

"You know I had nothing to do with Dan, right? Please tell me you know that."

Naomi ignored her. "Do you have a place to stay tonight?"

Jane shook her head.

"Okay, honey," Naomi said, throwing her arm around Jane's shoulder, "You can stay with me for a few hours, regroup, maybe catch some sleep. Then we'll head down to the station and I'll take you through all the BS procedure. I know it sucks, but my place is a little better than a holding cell."

The front door opened and an EMT backed out, wheeling along a gurney holding a black plastic body bag.

The body bag looked lumpy, uneven.

Jane's final memory of Dan, the love of her life: stuffed inside a lumpy black bag and being wheeled out of the home they shared together.

This thought brought on a fresh set of tears.

Why did she have to sleep? If she'd been awake, she might have been able to stop it.

You lost your husband because you had to nap.

You lost your niece because you couldn't face your fear, your illness.

You need to smarten up.

"Being here isn't going to do you any good," Naomi said, pulling Jane's face into her shoulder. "Why don't we head back to my place now?"

"I want to help them find Haley,"

"Almost every officer in town is searching the woods right now. They'll probably find her before the morning. And when they do, she's gonna need you." Naomi threw Jane a weak smile. "And you won't be any good to her if you're a tired, blubbering mess."

Jane pulled away, sniffling. "Can I get a few things first?"

"Of course, under my supervision."

One of the officers who helped the EMTs pull Dan's body out was now making his way back inside. Jane didn't recognize him. When he passed Naomi, she lightly touched his arm.

"Officer Grimes, would you mind escorting Mrs. Dalby and myself inside to gather a few things? She'll be staying with me tonight, if you're all done with her."

"Of course." Grimes smiled politely at Jane. "Follow me."

Jane stood up from the porch swing and followed the officer inside. When they crossed the threshold, she closed her eyes and gripped Naomi's hand.

"We're just going to go upstairs to my bedroom," Jane said.

Naomi understood. She led her upstairs carefully.

Don't open your eyes. Don't look at the blood, at the broken glass. Don't look.

At the top of the stairs, Jane opened her eyes. Naomi winked but still held her hand.

When they came to her room, Jane and Naomi walked in first, and Officer Grimes followed.

As she entered the room, Jane froze in mid-step.

Enoch was waiting for her.

He hugged the nightstand, looking at her with his big, tear-drenched eyes.

"Everything okay?" Grimes said.

"Honey." Naomi shook Jane's shoulder. "What's wrong?"

Enoch slammed his head into Dan's nightstand, rattling the picture of the happy family on top.

Jane looked at Naomi and Grimes, but their expressions were blank. How did they not notice this?

"I'm… fine," Jane said, letting go of her friend's hand.

She walked around the bed. Enoch tilted his head to stare at her, like a puppy.

Jane opened her closet and pulled a duffle bag from the top shelf. She unzipped it and put it on her bed.

If she'd known the previous night would be the last time she and her husband would ever share a bed again, she would have held him tighter while they slept. She would have kissed him every chance she had. She would have begged him to make love to her.

The monster hugging her husband's nightstand started to cry again. He opened his mouth to wail but hardly any sound escaped.

That made him frustrated, and he cried harder.

Jane opened her dresser drawers and collected enough clothes to wear for the next three nights, if need be.

"Any news downstairs?" Naomi said quietly to Grimes.

"Some, we have—"

Jane tried to listen, but Enoch slammed his head into the nightstand again. His eyes begged for attention. He cocked his head, motioning to the picture of when they went to the Bronx zoo.

"—probably a knife," Jane heard Grimes say.

She spun, "Knife?"

Grimes took a step back, "Yes, ma'am. At least that's what the detectives are thinking at this time."

Jane breathed in deep and looked at the ground, lost in thought. "Are you sure it wasn't an... *animal* that did this?"

"No, ma'am. The cuts look too clean to be an animal. That's what they say."

A tide of morbid relief washed over her for a moment. That meant it had to be a human that murdered Dan, and not the monster in her mind.

But the relief was short lived; Jane remembered Isaiah's claws.

Claws the shape of a kitchen knife.

"Everything okay, Mrs. Dalby?"

Enoch knocked his head into the nightstand again.

"Yes, I'm fine."

She walked over to Enoch, leaned over—careful not to touch him—and grabbed the picture frame.

"Are you happy now?" she whispered to him.

Enoch seemed fine for the moment. He stopped banging his head, but still cried.

Jane threw the picture into her duffle bag and rubbed her temples. Her head swam with ideas and nothing seemed to make sense. A headache was coming on.

Her gun sat on her nightstand where she had left it while waiting for the police to arrive. She reached for it, but Naomi's hand landed on it first.

"Maybe you should leave this home, honey."

"I need it."

"You'll be safe. You'll be with me."

"But I still need it."

Officer Grimes walked away slowly, not wanting to get involved.

Jane couldn't find a way to explain how the gun helped her headaches. Naomi would think she was insane, which she very well might have been, but she didn't need other people thinking that yet.

"Leave it, honey."

Jane felt violated. This was her gun, her life, her tumor, her dead husband, and her niece lost in the woods. Naomi had no right to interfere with any of it.

I'm still strong enough to handle a gun, dammit!

"Are you afraid of me?" Jane asked. "Afraid I'll shoot someone?"

"Hell, no," Naomi said. "I've seen you shoot."

Jane didn't smile back. "So why can't I have my gun?"

Naomi went to the duffle bag, zipped it shut, and grabbed it for Jane. She wrapped her arm around Jane's shoulder and led her to the door, where Grimes waited.

"Because, honey, you'll be staying with the best damn detective in this county."

"I can handle a gun. Don't treat me like a child. I was a cop once and had a badge, remember?"

"Honey, once a cop always a cop." She ushered Jane out of the room. "But if you really don't want to draw the wrong kind of attention, I'd leave it at home. For now."

Jane tried to protest; she needed to find the words, the courage, to show Naomi that she was responsible enough to handle her own damn firearm.

She glanced over her shoulder while walking out, trying to look at her gun, her only cure for her headaches. She locked eyes with Enoch again, who still banged his head miserably on the nightstand.

Grimes closed the door behind them, and Jane could hear the rhythmic *thumps* all the way down the hall.

The beginning of a headache rooted itself at the base of her brain and threatened to lock her head in a vice.

CHAPTER 4

Jane's mind swirled with grief and uncertainty. Naomi talked as they walked down the street, but her voice sounded far away, and Jane couldn't understand what Naomi said.

Jane's feet shuffled along the pavement. The forest, glimpsed between the houses they passed, stood dark and looming, holding onto its secrets.

Jane nearly collapsed into Naomi's arms.

"Haley," she said. "Haley is in there and she's scared."

Naomi tried to lift Jane, taking on her weight, but Jane pushed her away and insisted she walk on her own. Naomi said something in response, but Jane couldn't hear anything more than muffles.

When they entered Naomi's house, Jane had no trouble making herself at home. She staggered to the couch and plopped down, pressing her face against one of the throw pillows to hide her tears.

Naomi crouched down next to her and stroked her friend's hair.

I'm strong. Haley needs me.

But I can't do anything about it sitting here.

"I feel so hopeless," she said, turning her head to Naomi. "I don't like it."

"I know, honey," Naomi rubbed her back. "But we have to let the professionals do their job."

"Are you going to help look?"

"Of course,"

"When?"

"I'm on duty tomorrow," Naomi said. "I'm sure they'll find her by then, but I'll be there to make sure the sonovabitch that did this gets the shit kicked out of him."

"Okay."

"No, I promise you, I'm going to hit him so hard his children will be born bruised."

"I believe you."

"You better. He'll be picking up his broken teeth with broken fingers."

Jane allowed herself to smirk.

Naomi leaned back and sat on her butt, pushing her legs out in front of her. She held Jane's hand.

Cops usually had one of two sets of eyes: eyes that always leered at you, making you feel as if you'd done something wrong, or they had kind eyes, soft eyes, and they looked at you with a limitless amount of understanding.

Naomi had the latter, and it never failed to make Jane feel comfortable.

"How about I make you a cup of tea?"

Jane sat up. "That sounds good. But let me make it."

"Are you kidding?"

"You've done so much for me already. Just relax and let me make it."

"Sit your skinny ass down," Naomi said. "You've been through enough. Just relax."

"Naomi, let me do something. If I don't do something useful, I feel like I'm going to go insane. I feel useless and hopeless, like one of those sick people who can't do anything without help anymore. I'm not dead *yet!*"

The words echoed in her mind: *I'm not dead yet.*

Jane stood and walked past Naomi, who didn't try to stop her. Her breath came and went in rapid hitches, and she was unable to catch it. She pressed a hand to her head.

"This damn headache," Jane sobbed.

"Okay." Naomi rose and hugged Jane. "I guess no tea then. How about we see what's on TV? You know, something to take your mind off... this."

Jane lifted her face from Naomi's shoulder. Farther back in the house was the kitchen window. Jane focused her eyes through the tears.

A figure looked in at them.

"Naomi," Jane said softly.

"How about a comedy? You make the popcorn, I'll pop in the movie?"

"Naomi," she said again.

The figure on the other side of the window pushed its gnarled hands against the glass and breathed a thick cloud of steam. Jeremiah scrawled on the foggy glass with a shaking finger. He worked quickly, but sloppily, the way a child might write.

MONSTER

Naomi followed Jane's stare and looked to the window and then back at Jane.

"What's wrong, honey?"

Jane shook off her trance. "It's nothing, I guess I'm just tired."

Naomi gave her a nervous, but polite smile. "So how about we watch TV?"

"Actually, I don't think so tonight. I should probably get some rest."

Naomi must have sensed something, her expression turned sour.

"I think you should stay with me. You shouldn't be alone right now."

"I'll be fine. Please. I just need to be by myself for a bit." Jane tried to match Naomi's soft, sympathetic eyes. "I hope you understand."

Naomi sighed. "Okay. Get some rest. We'll start fresh tomorrow. I promise everything will be okay. Do you want to take the bed and I'll sleep on the couch?"

"No!" Jane's voice snapped, and she quickly caught herself. "You take the bed. I prefer the couch anyway. Please."

To prove her point, Jane plopped on the couch and threw both her legs up, letting out an exaggerated sigh.

This is stupid. I'm stupid. But Naomi isn't stupid. She knows something is up.

"Okay, couch it is then. I'll go up and grab you the extra blanket."

Jane was about to protest, but that might raise even more suspicion, so she kept quiet.

When Naomi made it all the way up the stairs, Jane jumped up from the couch and rushed to the kitchen window.

Jeremiah wasn't there. But his word was, still on the glass, in fading letters.

MONSTER

Of course, Isaiah is a monster.

It took my niece.

It killed the only man I loved.

She balanced on her tiptoes and peered out the window. The letters were mostly gone now, and she had a better glimpse of outside.

No Jeremiah.

What did he want from her?

The sound of Naomi's feet thudded down the stairs.

Jane ran back to the living room and crouched near her duffle bag. She unzipped it and pretended to go through it.

She found the picture of Dan, Haley, Sarah, and herself. She wanted to cry again, but had neither the tears nor the energy for it.

"Got the blanket," Naomi said.

"Thanks." Jane took the blanket and held it close to her chest.

A long, uncomfortably empty silence passed between them before Jane broke it.

"Well, goodnight."

"Goodnight, Jane," Naomi said, retreating to the stairs.

After a few steps, she hesitated.

"Jane?" Naomi said. "Just know that I'm here for you if you need me. Anytime. Don't hesitate to wake me up or anything. I'll always be here and ready to talk. We'll get this all figured out. Trust me. Tomorrow, you and I will head down to the station. We'll take care of whatever bullshit paperwork we need to, and I'm sure by then Haley will be found. Safe."

"Thank you," Jane said. "I don't know what I'd do without you."

Naomi nodded and walked up the stairs, out of sight.

Jane looked to the ceiling, holding her breath, listening for Naomi's footfalls. She had a general idea of where her bedroom was, and once Jane was sure that Naomi was snug in bed, she went back to the kitchen window.

Jeremiah waited there now, blowing steam on the glass. He looked more tired than usual. Heavy bags hung beneath his sunken eyes. Jane shared his fatigue. He scrawled a new word on the steamed glass.

HELP

In the years Jane had been followed by Jeremiah, he never once tried to communicate with her this way. How could he even spell?

He's a part of me, Jane reminded herself.

"What do you want?" She whispered.

Jeremiah looked at her with puzzlement, then he leaned forward and breathed a fresh billow of steam on the glass.

FOLLOW

"Follow? Follow you?"

Jeremiah nodded.

How could she trust him? Was he one of her usual monsters that stayed as a figment of her imagination? Or was he something worse, like Isaiah.

"Where's Haley?" Jane said softly, yet firmly.

Jeremiah floated away from the window and to the back door of the house. Jane leaned on the counter and pressed her face against the windowpane. She watched the monster bend down and wrap his lips around the outside doorknob.

Jane glanced to the door; a milky wisp of steam came through the deadbolt, turning it with an audible click.

Jane went to the door and touched the deadbolt, testing to see if it had indeed opened.

Did he just do that?

Or was it unlocked the entire time?

She opened the door.

Jeremiah waited on the other side of the threshold, feet never touching the ground, levitating, drifting.

He beckoned her to follow him.

"Okay," she whispered, "but first I need to get my gun."

He tipped his head in a bow of agreement.

CHAPTER 5

*O*f course Jeremiah didn't open the door. I did that myself. It's all a
hallucination. That's what Jeremiah is... a hallucination.

Jane repeated the word to herself so many times it became a
personal mantra: *hallucination.*

But after everything she'd seen today, how could she really
be sure what was true and what was not?

Jane crept through the back yards of her neighbors, trying
to stay out of the light and using the cover of trees whenever
possible. If Naomi saw or heard her, she would drag her back
and wouldn't let her out of her sight. Guilt pressed at Jane,
leaving Naomi like that, especially after she put so much trust
in her.

Jeremiah stayed farther behind, only moving whenever
Jane did. Sometimes she would check back and make sure he
still followed, but he was always there, and he seemed grateful
for the attention. He puffed out steam as he floated through the
residential yards, like a macabre freight train.

The air had grown cool, and she hadn't brought a jacket with
her. She wore only her jeans and t-shirt. Her teeth chattered
from either the chill or nervousness.

In the woods behind the houses, she occasionally saw
flashes through the trees. The lights must've been from the
officers' flashlights, searching for her niece. Sometimes faint
voices or snippets of conversation made their way to her ears,
but the noises died away to silence quickly.

She was technically trespassing on her neighbors' properties.
She couldn't count the times she'd been sent on calls like
these—to investigate some creep in the back yards of residential
houses—when she was an active duty officer.

As she drew close to her home, she stopped and listened to the quietness. The woods were very still now, and the only noise came from the wind rushing through the leaves and trees.

She walked along the grassy path between two houses and out to the front sidewalk. There she continued the rest of the way to her home casually, carrying a façade of confidence.

Six empty police cars were parked outside her home. They belonged to the officers combing the woods, or investigating her home. Their reds and blues were off. An ambulance waited on standby. More personnel would be arriving soon. The murder of a cop and abduction of his niece didn't get the standard treatment. By sunrise, every cop in town would be on the case. Detectives and top brass would get involved. After that would be state police and FBI agents.

Officer Grimes sat on the stoop, catching a smoke. He stood up when he spotted Jane, threw the cigarette down, and snuffed it under the heel of his boot.

"Mrs. Dalby," he said, "I thought you went home with Detective Adler."

Nobody ever called Naomi by her last name. She preferred *Detective Naomi* whenever possible. He must be a rookie. Jane didn't correct him. That was his mistake to make and learn from.

"I did, but I needed to come back for my medication."

"Oh,"

"I'm sick. I have—"

"Brain cancer. I know."

Jane pursed her lips. "I was going to say pills. *I have pills* I need to take."

"I'm sorry, Mrs. Dalby," Grimes' face turned red. "I shouldn't have opened my mouth."

Damn right you shouldn't have.

"How did you know about that?"

When Jane had been diagnosed, she did her best to ensure the news would stay quiet. She only told her family and Naomi—she hadn't even told Naomi how bad things really were.

"Dan told us."

"Dan?"

Us?

"Yeah. Poor guy. He helped me so much, but I knew he was going through a lot. He did everything he could for you. It seemed like he really loved you. He was a good guy. I swear when I find the fucker that did this..." he trailed off.

Jane tightened her fists and willed herself not to cry again. Why did he know all this? Who else did Dan tell? She looked over her shoulder. Jeremiah wasn't there anymore.

"Can I please just go inside and get my medicine? I need to get back to Naomi."

"Mrs. Dalby, this is still an active crime scene."

"I'm aware, but I really need my medication. Detective Naomi gave me permission," she bit her bottom lip.

"She did? Let me contact her. I need to hear it from a superior. You understand."

"You really want to be the one to wake her up? Disturb her at home?"

Grimes paused, his hand hovering over his radio. His eyes narrowed at Jane for a few breathless moments before his mouth blossomed into a full smile. His shoulders slackened as he brought his hand away from the radio and rested it in his pocket. Jane allowed herself to relax.

"Okay, Mrs. Dalby," he said with half a chuckle. "Just be quick."

Grimes opened the door and allowed Jane to step inside her home.

Dan's blood was still soaking into the carpet. This area must've been photographed and searched for evidence already. However, it was silly of her to expect the blood would be gone. Officers don't clean up blood.

All that was left of her husband, her love, and her life for thirteen years had been reduced to a damp stain on her carpet.

Her stomach roiled and Jane turned her back to the stain. She climbed the stairs with only her gun and Haley on her mind.

Thunk

The sound echoed softly from directly down the hall. A hollow and distant noise. She looked behind her; Grimes climbed the stairs slowly.

Thunk Thunk

Grimes' expression remained stone-like and professional. He didn't appear to hear the noise.

Jane's insides turned cold; her limbs froze and locked up. Now she could hardly hear anything else, save for the blood pounding in her ears. She took a step, but it felt like slow motion.

It's Enoch.

Jane took the photograph from Dan's nightstand, like Enoch wanted. Why would he still be banging his head? Why couldn't he just leave her alone?

Because he's a monster.

With a weak tremble in her knees, Jane struggled to pick up the pace. She entered her room and shut the door behind her, locking it before Grimes had a chance to invite himself in.

Thunk

She whirled around. Enoch waited exactly where he always did. His eyes brightened at the sight of her. His dry, cracked lips spread into something desperate that once upon a time could have been considered a smile.

He'd been banging his head so hard he'd split his forehead open. A trail of scarlet blood traveled down his face, smearing into his left eye and continuing down his cheek, dripping off his chin and onto his bare, lesion-riddled chest.

He blinked away the blood, then sniffled, looking at Jane.

"What the hell did you do to yourself, Enoch?"

Jane went over to him and sat down on Dan's side of the bed. He looked so hopeless and lost. He needed her so badly.

Jane reached for him. She wanted to touch him, hold him, and wipe the blood from his eye. She wanted to cry with him, yet show him she was strong enough for the both of them.

She stopped before her hand touched his face.

He's not real.

She retracted her hand and looked down, shamefully.

Enoch's breaths quickened, and his chest heaved. He wanted her attention, her touch.

He threw his head back and slammed it into the drawer.

Jane jumped, her heart skipping a beat.

Enoch left an oval-sized imprint of blood on the oak wood.

He arched back, ready to slam into it again, when Jane put a hand on the metal handle.

Enoch stopped in mid-arch, every muscle in his body held taut.

Jane gripped the handle tighter and pulled the drawer open. Enoch relaxed a little. She slid the drawer open farther.

Enoch finally let go of the nightstand and whirled around, throwing himself onto the ground and crying while smiling. He still watched her.

Inside Dan's drawer lay an assortment of random things—a jar of Vaseline, a box of tissues, a penknife, a note pad, and an old box of condoms even though he rarely used them. Jane couldn't get pregnant. Even so, he hadn't touched her in over a year.

A small, black, metal box lay toward the back of the drawer, almost tucked away from sight. It looked like a gun safe, but Dan kept his gun safe in the closet.

She picked it up and felt its weight. Heavy.

When she shook it, nothing thumped or rattled. No gun inside.

She rolled the box in her hands, studying it. The lock looked bent, caved in on itself.

Enoch gestured for her to continue.

She dug her fingers under the lid of the box and started to pry it open. The broken lock gave way with a *snap!*

The lid flew open and small squares of paper slid out. Polaroid photographs. The box overflowed full of them.

Jane picked up a stack and fanned them in her hands, studying each one carefully. She dropped one and focused on the next. Again and again.

A fresh headache clouded over her brain like a fast-moving hurricane. She dropped all the photographs and crawled over the bed for her gun on her nightstand.

But halfway to her nightstand, she gave up and instead curled into a ball and cried.

CHAPTER 6

TWO YEARS AGO

Jane stared out the passenger-side window, watching the snow-covered trees pass in a blurry haze of white and brown and winter green.

Sarah sat next to her, eyes focused on the snow-masked road. Ever since they got back in the car together, she hadn't said a word, and seemed to be in a rush to get home.

Even while they were walking through the mall, buying Christmas gifts, Sarah remained reserved and unresponsive. She was miles away within her own head.

Jane needed to get out of the house to find Dan a Christmas gift, though at the time had no clue what to get him. She called her younger sister and persuaded her to drive them out to the mall together to shop for him.

He liked to cook, so she bought him new cookware—a pot, two pans, and a set of knives. She also bought him a teddy bear dressed as a police officer, which made her laugh, and was really more for her than him. She also splurged a little bit and bought him a bottle of single malt scotch. She didn't know much about scotch or any kind of whiskey, but the man behind the counter said this one was his personal favorite, very smooth.

A costly set of gifts, that far exceeded their agreed spending limit, but he was her everything. He was worth it.

She didn't know how much longer she would be around, and wanted to show him how much he meant to her while she still had the chance—while there was still a breath in her body, and a heartbeat in her chest.

In the mall, when Jane finally escaped from her sister, she

stealthily bought Sarah a pair of wine glasses engraved with a treble clef music note—at least that's what the salesperson told Jane, and knowing nothing about music, she had to take the salesperson's word for it. She also bought a small, leather-bound journal for her to write song lyrics in.

Sarah used to write songs and play guitar a lot, but ever since Haley was born, and Jonah—her ex-husband—left her, wanting nothing to do with her or the child, Sarah never had the time or energy to pursue it. Jane hoped this would give her hobby the jumpstart it needed.

For Haley, just seven years old, Jane bought a small bottle of perfume and a length of purple ribbon to wear in her hair.

The night air was cold, sharp as teeth. Even with her coat, scarf, and hat, Jane still shivered. She turned the car's heat up.

Still early in the night, the empty road stretched into darkness. Even though Christmas Eve waited just around the weekend, no one headed into the cold like this without a purpose. Jane found it peaceful, despite the chill.

"Maybe we should stop and get a pizza? I'm sure Dan and Haley would like some, too," Jane said, watching her older sister's reaction. "We could bring it back for them."

Sarah's face remained stone. "No. I think I would just like to get home."

"Why? We finally have the night away from our families. Don't you want to enjoy it just a little longer? It's just the two of us, how it used to be."

"I want to get back to Haley."

Jane touched her sister's hand. "I know you're worried about her, but don't be. Dan is watching her."

"That's what I'm worried about," Sarah said after a moment.

"Dan's a *police officer* for God's sake,"

I used to be one, too.

"It's not that."

Jane let go of her sister's hand and slumped against the passenger-side door. "So what is it then?"

Sarah held her breath, eyes darting over to Jane, clearly choosing her words carefully.

"The way he looks at her," Sarah said, finally.

"What about the way he looks at her?"

"I don't know. He stares at her sometimes and he watches the little things she does. Sometimes he sweats when he's around her."

"Maybe it's nerves. He's never really been around children before."

"I don't think so. You look into his eyes and you see anger and thirst. It scares the living shit out of me. I'm upset he's home with her. I'm sorry, but I needed to tell you this. You need to understand, Jane, that I wouldn't have even left the two of them alone together if I could help it."

"Are you really that worried?"

"I can't be mad at the babysitter for getting sick and canceling, but I'm allowed to be worried about my daughter. The way he makes her sit on his lap and tells her stories... I don't trust him."

Jane was about to tell her that Dan meant no harm, that he loved his niece more than anything, and neither of them would let anything bad happen to Haley.

But all Jane told her sister was, "WATCH OUT!"

Jane lunged for the steering wheel. There was something in the road: a massive figure with sharp claws that glinted in the white of the snow.

Jane twisted the wheel and the car veered to the right, and as she passed by the monster in the road, it turned its head to her. Six off-white lines ran up and down its maw, overlapping its lips and face.

Are those teeth!?

Jane was thrown forward, her seatbelt catching her by the chest. She felt strangely calm as the car struck a tree.

Sarah grunted.

The car's frame bent from the force with a groan of metal. The windshield cracked into a spider-web motif before shattering, spraying glass in her eyes and hair. The hood of the car crumpled inward, wrapping around the trunk of an oak tree in a twisted embrace.

Everything was quiet.

Jane blinked and touched her nose. Blood on her fingers, blood on her face.

Then the pain came. There was pressure on her face, and she knew instantly the cartilage in her nose had been crushed. She tried to breathe, but her lungs wouldn't gather any air. The taste of copper filled her mouth.

There was a tangle of branches and leaves where the windshield used to be.

She struggled around in her seat until she could look at her sister. She tried to call her name, but no sound came. Only a soft whisper managed to sneak from her lips.

"Sarah." Blood from Jane's nasal cavity bubbled out of her mouth, dribbled down her chin.

Sarah's head lay twisted toward her sister, eyes half closed, face peppered with shards of glass.

A tree branch had impaled the windshield, its tip lost within her sister's neck.

Jane tried the door; the handle worked but the door wouldn't open. The crash had jammed it, bending into the metal of the frame. Jane climbed through the broken passenger-side window, coughing blood onto the peppermint-colored snow.

She struggled through the window, inching herself almost to the ground before her muscles gave out, and gravity pulled her the rest of the way. She hit the ground hard and let out a sharp cry. Propping herself into a sitting position, she leaned against the door and ran her fingers through her hair, combing out the bits of glass.

She heard the monster before she saw it.

Snow crunched under its feet, yet it didn't leave any footprints. Its feet were tipped with black, mud-caked talons. The thing's chest and arms were muscled and broad.

The white lines on its face were indeed its teeth, rooted within its mouth, but the bottom set reached close to its eyes and the top set overlapped them, poking down past its chin.

The monster looked at her with a snarl, but as it focused on Jane's face and examined her wounds, its eyes softened. It crouched and leaned close to her face, sniffing.

Jane watched, helplessly. She'd been paralyzed with fear, unable to do anything but whimper. If the beast wanted to, it could have torn her to ribbons with its sharp, reflective claws.

In the back of her mind, Jane somehow recalled seeing shadows between trees, and outside of her home—shadows, she now remembered, about the size of this monster.

She'd been diagnosed with the cancerous brain tumor two months prior. Her doctor told her that a symptom of brain cancer could be hallucinations, causing her to see what he referred to as *shadow people.*

However, the doctor explained, sometimes—very rarely—the human mind will see the shadow people and acknowledge them, and give them faces and names. It's the brain's way of coping with something it doesn't understand, the same way that someone might see the face of the Virgin Mary in a piece of toast.

Though this was the first time Jane had ever locked eyes with this monster, she couldn't help but feel she'd seen it before, like a long-lost friend.

The monster rose and stalked away to the woods. It peered over its shoulder and looked at Jane.

She knew this wouldn't be the last time she'd see it.

Jane pushed her back flush with the car and tried to stand up. She rose to her feet and tried to stretch herself, but her neck, hips, and knees cracked loudly.

It seemed no one would be driving by anytime soon. She pulled her cellphone out of her pocket, but it read *No Service.*

Jane brushed off the seat of her jeans and staggered to the road. It was going to be a long walk.

She looked to Sarah, contorted in the driver's seat.

It was all Jane's fault.

She wanted to cry, but the tears wouldn't come.

As she walked, it felt as if someone were following her, keeping a protective eye over her. The monster was there, but always hidden.

Her sister's last words echoed in her mind: *"I don't trust him."*

CHAPTER 7

I don't trust him.

Jane slammed her fists on the mattress. A steady stream of drool pooled onto the fabric, but she didn't care.

Officer Grimes probably heard her crying, because he pounded on the door, demanding to be let in. But she didn't care about that either.

None of this was true. It couldn't be.

Dan was her husband, her best friend. They knew everything about each other. How could Dan keep a secret like this?

The tumor.

Maybe it wasn't real. Maybe the pictures were only a product of her tumor.

She rolled and looked over the edge of the bed, praying the pictures would no longer be there—that she'd simply made it all up in her diseased mind.

They were still there. Most were turned over, so the image was facing the floor.

Maybe the pictures themselves are there, but they're not of what I think they are. Maybe they're just harmless photos.

Maybe my brain hates me. It treats me like I'm a spider, and it's pulling off all my legs, watching me wiggle and tumble.

Jane steadied her breath. Her headache still pulsated at the stem of her brain, but for once she had something more important than her headache.

"Mrs. Dalby," Grimes' voice rang out from behind the door. "Open up, right now!"

Jane picked up the photograph and hesitated before turning it over in her hands.

Like a Band-Aid—do it quick.

She turned it over and pressed her hand to her mouth.

This wasn't a product of her tumor. This was a photograph from life.

The photo was of Haley. She looked seven or eight, Jane couldn't tell, but she was younger, naked. Jane saw small lumps—the beginnings of breasts—on her chest, purple and bruised around the nipples. Her eyes were red from too many tears. She was hunched over, trying to hide herself.

"I'm going to kick the door down, Mrs. Dalby!" Grimes said.

"I'm fine. Just give me a moment."

Jane looked at another photo.

Haley lay on the bed in this one, *Jane's bed*—the same bed she lay on now. The girl laid face down in the photograph, completely naked again, a man's hand pressed to her pale thigh. She recognized Dan's wedding ring.

So many pictures…

In the corner by the nightstand, Enoch lay against the wall, seemingly wheezing, though not making any sounds. Jane looked to him and he smiled thinly. He pointed to the photographs. He was sweating, and his chest heaved like he'd just run a marathon.

This is what he's been trying to tell me all along. It had nothing to do with the fucking picture of the Bronx Zoo.

The sheer stupidity of her misunderstanding filled her with the overpowering need to laugh, but everything else made her want to cry. The combination of the two emotions drove her to near insanity.

He was my love.

He was a monster.

Some part of her still hoped this was all a hallucination. She needed to talk to Haley, show her these pictures and ask if this was all true.

She needed to ask her why she didn't come to her, her aunt. She could have protected her if she'd known.

She needed to ask her how long her uncle had been doing this to her—if he'd been doing it at all.

No wonder Dan never touched me anymore.

But she couldn't ask her niece any of this, because some other monster had taken her.

Poor girl. Poor Haley. Jane had promised Sarah if anything were to happen to her, Jane would take care of Haley, raise her and look after her.

Good going, Jane. You can't do anything right. Thank God you aren't able to have kids, because you'd be a terrible mother.

You suck as an aunt.

You suck as a wife.

You suck as a sister.

You deserve this fucking tumor.

She leaned over from the bed and slammed her head into the nightstand, hoping that it would rattle her brain and shuffle her thoughts back to normal.

Instead, all it did was hurt a lot.

Damn! And how many times had Enoch done this?

The monster in the corner saw her wince in pain and crawled over to her, slowly, painfully. Hand over bony hand.

He inched his face toward hers. He already looked less pale and less gaunt. His sores were less inflamed. He'd been trying to tell Jane for so long, and now that he did, it looked like a weight had been lifted from his shoulders.

"How did you know?" Jane said to him. "I didn't even know."

Enoch tilted his head.

No, Dan couldn't have done this. He was an officer of the law.

But he never wanted to touch me. Not since Haley moved in with us.

"Enoch," Jane said, as his eyes brightened. "Are these photographs real? Did Dan really do this?"

He pointed to the photos and nodded.

Jane shuddered.

"Where did Isaiah take my niece? Where's Haley?"

Enoch frowned. He inched away and started to rise.

The two years he spent hunched over had really taken its

toll. He rose up, knees cracking, wobbling to find balance. His spine rolled up, each vertebrae resonating with a deep crack as they snapped into place.

She'd only seen him stand up once, when they'd first met. Back then, he moved much more horribly, more painfully. Now, he moved without pain, but also without confidence in his steps.

He staggered over to the other side of the room, each step taken as if the floor was covered with shards of broken glass.

He lifted his thin, sinewy arm and pointed to the window.

Jane got up from the bed and went over to him. When standing, Enoch towered over her by nearly two feet.

The blinds to the window were closed. Enoch cocked his head, encouraging her to open them.

She grabbed the pull-string and yanked them open.

It took a moment for Jane's eyes to adjust to the darkness outside. She squinted, gazing down into her yard.

Isaiah stood in her back yard, staring up at the window.

The darkness hid most of its features, but it was Isaiah

No sign of Haley.

Isaiah's savage eyes narrowed on Jane.

Grimes hammered at the door.

"Open up now, Mrs. Dalby!"

The monster in her yard breathed in deep and exhaled a white plume of breath from its nostrils.

Jane broke eye contact with it. She turned away, leaving Enoch still pointing out the window, smiling.

She picked up the photographs and stuffed them back in the lock box, and slid it back in Dan's nightstand drawer.

This isn't true. It can't be.

Before opening the door for Grimes, she walked around the bed and grabbed her gun from her table. She shoved it into the waistband of her jeans and pulled her shirt over it, trying to conceal the bulge.

She took a deep breath and opened the door.

"Care to tell me what the hell that was about?" Grimes asked, his eyes darting around the room.

"I'm sorry about that. I'm so sorry."

"Did you forget how to work a door?"

"No, officer."

"Really? Because I'm pretty sure I was telling you to let me into the room."

"I'm sorry, I just got so—"

"So you think the best thing to do was closing the door in the officer's face who is helping you out by doing this? Is that right?"

"Officer, please—"

"I heard crying."

Jane looked down, shameful. "Yeah, that was me."

"Everything all right?"

"Fine. I should really get back to Naomi."

She tried to squeeze past him, but he blocked her.

"Wait. I just wanted to tell you that I'm sorry about Dan," he whispered.

"That's fine."

"He taught me a lot. Kinda took me under his wing when I joined the force. It breaks my heart. You know?"

"I know," she tried to move past him again, but he held still.

"He was such a good guy. He cared so much about you and," he paused again, then smiled, *"Haley."*

The way he said her niece's name—as if he could taste the word on his lips—made Jane's stomach churn.

He removed his hat and held it to his chest, trying to show respect. His manners altered, as if he'd transformed into an entirely different person.

Was it Jane's imagination, or did a long, black tongue slide out of Grimes' mouth and run along his lips?

Her temples began to throb, heralding the onset of another headache.

"Mrs. Dalby," he said, with an air of smugness, "where's your gun?"

Her heart skipped a beat.

"I put it away. Locked it up and put it in my closet. You know, trying to be safe."

Grimes threw his head back and laughed.

"Always so smart," he said, "even when you're *dying* you still think about the safety of others."

Jane's eyes widened.

"I'm sorry," Grimes continued, "I didn't mean to speak out of turn. Sometimes I just talk and don't even realize it."

Nothing about his body language indicated he was sorry.

Jane shifted from foot to foot, uncomfortably. If she were to dash past him, would he try to stop her?

Grimes must have realized she was looking for a way out; he stepped to the side of the threshold and smirked.

Jane didn't hesitate. She sped past him and down the hall, not looking back, even when Grimes said: "Tell Naomi I said 'Hi', would you?"

She ran down the stairs, taking them two at a time.

How did he know?

What did he know?

She turned to go into the kitchen but spotted Dan's bloodstain. She'd gathered the courage to walk past it but then saw two other officers standing in her back yard, shining their lights over what used to be her glass door.

No sense in talking a risk talking to other officers. Whom could she trust now?

Upstairs, a police radio buzzed. Grimes talked into it, but his words were mumbled and quiet.

She spun around and exited through her front door.

The night air hit her with a chilly breeze. It caressed her face and wisped through her hair, and it felt good.

Soon she wouldn't feel the breeze anymore. Wouldn't feel anything anymore.

Grimes' words echoed in her ear, reminding her of the slow approach of her own death.

As if I needed reminding.

She trotted down the stairs to her front porch and wrapped around the side of the house.

Isaiah wasn't there anymore, but the officers still were.

Deeper in the woods, she saw flashlights from some of the search party. Then she saw something else. It was difficult to tell in the darkness, but it looked like smoke rising from behind the tree trunks.

Not smoke… steam.

As if on cue, Jeremiah floated out from behind the trees. His bright yellow hair poked out first, followed by the rest of him. He stayed only long enough to gather her attention and then drifted back into the woods.

She crouched low and ran to him, as quietly as possible.

CHAPTER 8

Pain exploded behind Jane's eyes, spreading like wildfire through her brain.

She tried to follow Jeremiah, but couldn't. She leaned against the trunk of a maple tree and tried to stifle her coughs. Her stomach roiled and she leaned over to vomit, but only dry-heaved. There was no food in her stomach to be puked back up.

She quickly dug in her waistband for the gun and shoved its barrel into her mouth. As the cold steel scraped against her teeth, the pain leaked away to a dull throb.

Jane liked the throbbing sensation sometimes—the steady pulsating reminded her that her heart was still beating, that she wasn't dead yet.

Who needs fucking aspirin when you have a Smith & Wesson that works just as well?

However, some part of Jane knew if she were to inch her finger over a little bit and gave the trigger a squeeze, all of her pain would be gone forever. No more headaches, or tumors, or monsters.

That was the exact reason she kept the damn thing unloaded, to prevent thoughts like that from invading her mind.

If Isaiah tries to touch me or Haley...

Up ahead, officers talked in code. Their radios buzzed in and out and they laughed and joked and tried to make light of the fact that searching through the words for a lost child would be the high point of their entire night.

Jane had been on calls like this before, and officers needed to laugh to keep the grim reality at bay. They joked to stave off depression or sadness or to keep focused while knowing they were likely searching for a corpse

Jane shuddered.

Jeremiah waved his arm frantically, urging Jane to keep the pace. She pulled herself upright, slipped the gun back in her waistband, and dashed to the next tree where Jeremiah waited. There, she sat down in a pile of leaves and tried to spit the sour taste of bile from her mouth.

At the maple tree where Jane had just left, an officer shined his light directly on the scuffs of her footprints, freshly pressed into the dirt.

Jeremiah was now a couple feet ahead of her, behind another tree. He held up a hand as if signaling for her to stop. His eyes never looked directly at the police officers, though Jane didn't doubt he knew each one's exact location.

If Jeremiah was a projection of Jane, like she'd been led to believe, then how did he know where the officers were? And how did Enoch know about the pictures in Dan's drawer?

It was useless for Jane to try to make sense out of it. She'd already fallen down the rabbit hole, and to find her way out she needed to play by these monsters' rules.

Jeremiah waved her over and she ran low, like she'd been trained to do.

When she reached him, her feet slipped out from under her, and she slid, ramming her shoulder into the tree trunk and sending lightning bolts of pain up her back and neck. Jeremiah dipped low and put a thin, bony finger to his lips.

Steam filtered to the right and left of his finger as he shushed her.

An officer poked his head around the tree, his flashlight sweeping left and right.

"See something?" a gravel-voiced officer said.

"I thought I heard something," the officer near Jane said.

Jane recognized that gravel voice as Officer Gunther. She had never worked with him directly, but had seen him enough times at the station and on calls to grow accustomed to his voice. The other officer didn't sound familiar.

But he was close to her.

Jane closed her eyes and held her breath, wondering briefly if her thundering heartbeat was audible.

The officer sighed, and the sound of broken twigs indicated his departure from the tree.

Jane exhaled the fire in her lungs. She opened her eyes and wiped the sweat off her forehead with her T-shirt.

"This is stupid," the officer said, his voice diminishing in the distance. "She's not here."

You're not searching deep enough. Why are you still looking so close to the house? Haley could be farther away by now.

Jeremiah rose above her, his thin fingers making the shape of a gun. He kept his eyes on Jane, waving his finger gun around.

Jane pulled her gun out of her waistband and showed it to Jeremiah.

"This?" she whispered.

Jeremiah nodded and then pointed to the ground where she sat. The roots of the maple tree bulged from the ground, like knuckles gripping the earth.

He pointed to a specific spot—a pocket between two roots.

Jane placed the gun in the alcove and looked up to Jeremiah for reassurance.

He nodded and beckoned her to follow.

"But I need my gun."

Without the gun in hand, a little spark of a headache already ignited deep in her brain.

Jeremiah shook his head and waved her forward again. He turned around and floated to the next tree a couple of yards away.

Reluctantly, Jane stood up, rubbed her shoulder, and followed.

She'd barely hit the halfway mark before something slammed into her and pummeled her to the ground.

Thick fingers wrapped around the back of her head and pushed her face into the dirt. A knee dug against the top of her spine. She gasped to speak, to scream, but only inhaled grass and leaves and dirt.

"Stay down!" Gunther said.

She swallowed and a warm lump of dirt and saliva slid down her throat.

"You got her?" another voice said.

"Yeah, come help me out."

The click and rattle of handcuffs preceded her arms being forcefully yanked behind her. The cuffs clicked into place, digging into the flesh of her wrists.

Fuck, this hurts. No wonder people resist.

They patted their hands over her back, in her pockets, under her belly, between her legs.

"All right, she's clear, let's stand her up."

The two officers pulled Jane first to her knees, then to her feet. She blinked the dirt from her eyes and spat out the filth from her mouth.

"Officers, it's me. It's Jane Dalby," she wheezed as she drew a breath.

"We know," said Gunther.

The other officer pressed his radio, confirming to dispatch Mrs. Dalby was in custody.

"No," Jane said, shaking her head, words coming out weakly, "you're looking for Haley. Find her. Find my niece."

The world seemed to tilt. Trees spun and shifted. The officers dragged her along, not caring if she kept her balance or not.

"We'll find your niece," Gunther said, "but right now we need to deal with you."

They reached Naomi's house and led her up the walkway. Inside, three other officers waited in the kitchen. Grimes leaned against the wall with his arms crossed and the ghost of a smirk still on his face. On the floor next to him sat a bulging black garbage bag.

Naomi sat at the table with her head in her hands. Her outfit remained the same, with the new addition of her badge hanging around her neck, and the kit belt around her waist holding her gun and cuffs.

Embarrassment rolled through Jane. Naomi trusted her, and now she had to see her like this. She had let her down. If only Naomi could understand why. If only she could explain the monsters. Naomi lifted her head and her eyes widened with surprise. She shot straight up from her chair.

"Holy hell, guys, why is she in cuffs? I told you to find her—not cuff her."

"Grimes mentioned she might be armed," Gunther said.

Naomi glanced to Grimes and then to Jane.

"Well, clearly she's not. Uncuff her. Show her some respect, please. She's not under arrest... yet."

Gunther sighed and worked on the cuffs. They loosened with a small ratcheting sound and Jane's hands were free. She rubbed her wrists, inspecting them for damage. A little red, but the skin remained unbroken.

Naomi looked at the other officer. "Can you at least get her a paper towel so she can clean herself up?"

The officer went to the kitchen sink and started looking, his hands straight down at his sides, as if afraid to touch anything. He ripped a couple of sheets off the roll, crumpled them up and gave them to Jane.

He wouldn't look at her while he handed them off.

"Sit down, Jane," Naomi said, pulling out a chair for her.

She did as she was told. She put the ball of paper towels on the table and laid them out, flattening them, one by one before pressing the sheets to her face.

"I hope you know I can arrest you right now for interfering with an investigation. You know that, don't you? Hell, I think I should."

Jane nodded, the simple motion making her dizzy. Her head sang with pain.

"Okay," Naomi continued. "I was asked to assist with this investigation, but my pull only reaches so far. So now let me ask you this, what the hell were you thinking? Why did go out on your own?"

"Haley..." was all Jane could say.

"Listen to me, Haley will be fine. You just need to trust us to do our jobs. Do you have any idea how damn suspicious this looks?"

"Suspicious how? I didn't—"

"That's something else we need to talk about," Naomi looked to Grimes.

He picked up the garbage bag and hefted it onto the table.

"Grimes told me that after you left he found these in your room."

Both Naomi and Grimes leaned away, watching Jane. The bag wasn't sealed completely; its tie-strings were loose, showing a small opening.

Jane slowly stood up, unsure of herself, unsure of the people around her, and spread the bag open.

Inside the bag were clothes—a blue tank top and black shorts—the same clothes she had set out for herself earlier, before she took a nap.

But these clothes were damp.

Jane rubbed the wetness between her fingers. She brought the shirt farther out of the bag and into the light.

She gasped when she saw the blood—Dan's blood. Somehow she knew it was his.

She dropped the shirt into the bag and sat back, gasping, tears welling in her eyes. She grabbed the paper towels and rubbed the blood off her hands. Panic rattled inside her mind, inside her chest, promising to drive out all reason if she did not get it under control. She forced herself to breathe in deeply through her nose, hold it, and breathe out through her mouth.

"You are now under arrest for the murder of Dan Dalby." Naomi said, eyes hardening, lips thinning. "You have the right to remain silent. Anything you say can and will be used against you in a court of law. You have the right to an attorney. If you cannot afford an attorney, one will be appointed to you. Do you understand your rights?"

Jane had repeated those exact words countless times before, but hearing them spoken to her caused the blood to drain from her face. Her ears and cheeks burned. Her bottom lip quivered. She wanted to cry more than anything. She wanted to fall into a fit of sobs and stay there until all of this madness went away. Until she woke up, and Dan was alive and innocent and cooking breakfast, and Haley was back home, and Jane had a job to go to, and still had a full life ahead of her. Back when there was no such thing as monsters.

"I don't—I didn't, please."

"You'll come with me. We just want to bring you in. I am so sorry."

"But Haley…"

"Don't worry about her. We still have a search crew out there, and they'll continue looking 'til morning. But right now, you have a lot of explaining to do. Come on, honey."

Naomi stood and circled behind Jane. She rubbed her shoulders lightly, comforting her, while still urging her to come with her.

In the corner of her kitchen, Grimes grinned, no longer trying to conceal it.

"Son of a bitch!" Jane screamed. "You fucking planted those clothes there, didn't you?"

Grimes raised his hands in a mock surrender.

"Come on," Naomi said, "we're not doing this now, come with me."

Then she added, so quietly Jane almost didn't hear her: "I'm the best chance you've got."

She ushered Jane up from her chair, took her through the living room, past the dry bloodstain, and out the front door.

Naomi's sedan blocked Jane's driveway.

When they were a reasonable distance from the house, Naomi nudged Jane. "I would put the cuffs on you, but I'm afraid you might get turned on."

Jane fought back a smile. "Are you serious right now?"

"Come on, honey, just trying to make the best out of this situation. Look, I think you're innocent, but something like those clothes... we can't just pretend we never saw them."

"They're not mine." Jane stopped herself, gathered her thoughts, and started again. "I mean, they're my clothes, but the blood... It can't be. Someone had to set it up like that. I wasn't even in the same room when—"

"I know, honey, I know. That's why we're going down to get it all sorted out."

"But I can't leave Haley. She needs me! I found some things about her... about Dan. I need her back."

Naomi pulled Jane by the arm, so she stood in front of her. She pressed her against the cruiser.

"Anything in your pockets?" Naomi said.

Jane dug into the pockets of her jeans, pulled out a few loose tissues and eleven cents in spare change, piling it all neatly onto the hood of the car.

"Is that it?" Naomi said.

Jane nodded. Tears made hot tracks down her cheeks. She ransacked her brain, trying to find the words to explain to Naomi about the pictures, about Isaiah, but she couldn't, for even she was not sure what all of this meant.

Or why Isaiah wanted Haley.

"Turn your pockets inside out, honey."

Jane did.

Naomi bent down and squeezed Jane's ankles. Her hands worked up her calves and thighs, squeezing, moving the fabric of her jeans. She ran the back of her hand over Jane's crotch, even though it lasted a half a heartbeat, it was enough to spill fresh tears from Jane's clenched eyes.

"Hands behind your back." Naomi said.

Jane heard the clicking of handcuffs, felt Naomi's fingers against her wrist. Then, as the cool metal touched one of her wrists, Jane dropped and twisted.

Her fist slammed into Naomi's gut, and as she struggled to inhale, Jane karate-chopped her windpipe. Naomi convulsed, instinctively letting go of Jane and bringing her hands to her throat, clawing for breath.

Jane picked the handcuffs up and locked one side around Naomi's wrist and wrapped the other side around the handle of the door.

"I'm sorry, Naomi, I'm so damn sorry,"

With Naomi still stunned, Jane reached into her kit belt and snatched the handcuff key away. In less than ten minutes Jane would be long gone and it wouldn't matter anyway, but it still felt right to do.

"I promise I'll explain this all eventually. You just have to trust me right now. I'm the only one who can help Haley. These are my monsters. Not yours."

She ran around the font of the car as Naomi still battled for breath.

She took off, cutting across her neighbor's yard.

The blaring honk of a car horn ripped through the night.

She turned around. Naomi had the driver's door ajar,

enough to slide half her body inside. She leaned backward and laid on the car horn with the heel of her boot, producing one long headache-inducing stream of noise.

Several of her neighbors' lights switched on in their homes, if they hadn't already been awakened by the police activity.

Grimes bolted out of the front door, spotted Naomi struggling in the car, and followed her gaze to Jane.

Jane held still, caught like a deer in headlights.

Grimes' eyes sent a chill through her body. He abandoned Naomi's cry for help and instead focused on Jane, walking to her steadily, casually.

Jane broke into a run for the tree line and he did the same.

Only he was much quicker.

CHAPTER 9

Jane dashed through the forest, the trees looking familiar yet disorienting. She had no idea where she was going. The darkness made it difficult to navigate.

As she passed by a tree, she caught a glimpse of the tall yellow-haired figure, Jeremiah. He levitated in the air a couple dozen yards from her, waving his arms in the soft, invisible current that held him.

Jane turned abruptly, almost lost her footing, and changed course toward Jeremiah.

Her breath rushed from her lungs as she was hit from behind, a brute force knocking her forward. She lost her balance, collided with a tree, spun off, and tumbled to the forest floor.

Within seconds he was on top of her, picking her up by the hair. She screamed but Grimes punched her in the stomach, hard. Her breath abandoned her, and when she tried to speak, no sound came out.

She hit the ground again and clutched her stomach, rolling from side to side.

"Dumb bitch," Grimes said, circling her, like a vulture.

He kicked, but stopped his foot too soon, not connecting with her head, but kicking up dirt and grit into Jane's face.

Jane turned over onto her stomach and started her crawl. Jeremiah waited just ahead by the maple tree, watching her with concerned eyes.

"I swear to God, I'm going to make you pay for what you did to Dan."

"I didn't do anything to him," Jane said, still finding her breath.

Grimes should have had her cuffed by now. What was he

waiting for?

He's not waiting for anything. He wants to hurt me.

Jane crawled hand over hand, slowly moving to the maple tree.

With a running start, he kicked Jane's face.

Her head snapped back. Her front two teeth bent inward at the roots and popped off in her mouth.

She tasted blood.

He stepped back, breathed in deeply, and drew his gun. His eyes burned into her, but his voice remained cool and collected.

"I really should kill you, you know that, don't you?"

Jane dragged herself to the tree.

"I *could* kill you," he aimed his gun at her.

Jane's fingers dug between the roots of the tree.

"But I don't see the sense in killing you," he continued. "Why am I going to risk my job and waste a bullet on a bitch that's already half in the grave?" He lowered his gun. "When the cancer finally takes you, you're going to cry like a child, and no one is going to be there to hold you, because you killed the only man who'll ever love your dying ass."

Jane wrapped her fingers around the gun handle and brought it up. As an officer, Jane had been trained to aim for center mass, as it held the best chance of doing damage and neutralizing the enemy. Cops never aimed for the head because the margin for error was too wide.

But Jane didn't feel much like a cop right now—she aimed for his head and fired three shots before his eyes even registered something being wrong. The first shot hit him in the nasal cavity, sending him back into a tree. The second shot went wide, and the third struck his neck and continued upwards, exiting the back of his skull.

His throat blossomed like a new flower.

The tree behind him dripped with the hamburger meat that used to be his brain.

Jane's body tingled with energy. She kept the gun aimed, shaking. She'd let go of everything she'd been holding on to: every night Dan didn't want her in bed, every doctor's visit, and every monster. She didn't need to think about it, because when she fired the gun, the world ceased to exist for one beautiful moment.

Grimes crumpled in on himself and hit the ground. His wounds smoked as the shots echoed away.

Every officer in a mile radius heard those shots. She needed to get moving.

She sat up, turned over onto her knees, and coughed out her blood and teeth. She opened her mouth and tried to examine the damage, fingering the raw nerves. The pain caused her to wince as tears welled up in her eyes. Using the tree for balance, she slowly made her way to her feet.

The first time she'd fired her gun in two years. Hell, it was the first time she'd ever fired her gun *at* someone.

No more imaginary monsters. Jane killed a *real* man.

Why did he think I killed Dan?

He lay sprawled on the ground with his mouth open and his tongue hanging out. She rubbed her eyes with the palms of her hands. The same, long black monstrous tongue Jane thought she saw back at the house protruded from his mouth and hung from the side of his cheek.

She studied the dead man a little while longer, hoping that she would find some flaw in her mind's logic.

It's not his tongue hanging from his mouth, long and black like that, it's simply his blood.

But it didn't look like blood.

The sounds of shouting police officers broke the peaceful silence of the woods once more, reminding Jane she didn't have the time to ponder every little fallacy her tumor-addled mind threw at her.

Grimes wanted to hurt her, plain and simple. It had been self-defense.

Jeremiah floated in front of her vision to get her attention. He spun around her, locking his sympathetic eyes with hers.

It looked like he felt sorry for her.

"What do you want?" Jane said, walking ahead of him.

He stopped in front of her. Jane still walked, and he floated backwards, not taking his eyes away.

Her head pounded like some rock and roll drummer was in there, playing their favorite song. Each throb radiated down to her blood-soaked gums, vibrating the nerves where her front teeth used to be.

She brought the gun to her mouth, expecting her headache to go away, but instead burned herself on the hot barrel.

"Fuck!" She quickly pulled the gun out.

She swooshed blood and saliva around her mouth, coating her tongue, trying to cool the burn.

Jeremiah moved close to her face, begging her with his eyes to look at him.

"What? I don't want to see you right now. You let me be caught by them. I had to kill a man because of you."

Her words came out a little mumbled from her lack of teeth and the blister forming on her tongue. She wondered if Jeremiah could still understand her.

As if an answer to her question, he moved his fingers to the shape of the gun.

"Yes, you helped me hide the gun, but so fucking what. I was safe behind that tree until you made me follow you. Why couldn't I just stay there? Huh?"

Jeremiah looked down with sad eyes. He frowned and floated from her front to back, shamefully.

He clearly felt bad. Maybe he didn't know what he did was wrong.

Or maybe you're fucking crazy for trying to have a conversation with a projection of yourself. They lock people away for that.

They also lock people away for killing an officer.

"Okay, Jeremiah, fine. I don't care about that right now. Do you know where Haley is?"

Jeremiah drifted over to her front again. Jane stopped walking.

"Haley, my niece. Do you know where she is?"

Jeremiah cocked his head, confused.

Jane paused, thinking for a moment. She spat out a thick glob of blood. "All right. Take me to Isaiah."

Jeremiah smiled, steam blew out from his nose and between his jagged teeth in excitement. He rose higher off the ground and led the way deeper into the maze of woods and leaves and shadows.

CHAPTER 10

There has to be something I'm missing.

Jane ran through the woods, her shoulders sideswiped the tree trunks and branches her eyes hadn't seen coming. Not even the moon's light could pierce the canopy of thick forest Jeremiah led her deeper into.

Jane didn't think she'd ever been this far into the woods before. She might have been on calls for missing children, like Haley, where they would search the woods, but usually the children were found within a mile or two of their home.

She'd easily traveled three miles into the woods and her heart jackhammered in her chest. Her sweat-drenched clothes matted to her body. The wetness brought the chill deeper into her muscles. She struggled to keep up with Jeremiah.

Her legs felt like lead weights, and her thoughts drifted to a scene from a memory, where on a cold winter's night, Isaiah made his first appearance and caused the car to crash. And caused the death of Haley's mother. It was not lost on Jane that if Isaiah wasn't in the road that night, Sarah would still be alive, and Haley wouldn't have moved in with them. And she wouldn't be missing right now. It seemed to be more than a coincidence. Be it from coincidence or something larger, all of these events did indeed happen, and Jane needed to fix it all before her own clock ran out.

If these monsters are projections of me, of my personality, then how do they know more than me? How does Jeremiah know to go farther in the woods than I've ever gone?

And how did Enoch know about Dan's pictures, even when I'd spent thirteen years getting to know the man inside and out?

She'd been through Dan's nightstand a thousand times, but never once encountered a lock box or Polaroid pictures.

Ahead, Jeremiah seemed to maneuver between the trees with expert grace. Steam flowed steadily from him, and occasionally the clouds would envelop Jane, temporarily blinding her. It's not like it mattered: darkness or steam or a crystal-clear day, Jane would still feel lost and alone.

Her thoughts returned to the secrets monsters kept. If he knew more than her, why did he allow her to be captured by the other police officers?

Perhaps it was the same reason Enoch told her about the pictures and why Isaiah took her niece.

And even why Grimes tried to kill her.

The monsters are fucking with me.

The revelation hit her hard. Jane slowed to a steady pace, and then stopped running altogether, allowing Jeremiah to continue without her. She pressed her back against a tree trunk and held her stomach to stop it from trembling.

The pictures weren't real. It was all the construction of her brain. The photos were planted, like a seed, to make her lose trust in Dan. But it wouldn't work. Jane was smarter than that.

Jeremiah hadn't been leading her anywhere in particular, except maybe farther away from Haley.

They were all working together to let Isaiah steal Haley. These monsters were as real as the darkness that surrounded her, and they used her own fragile brain as a tool against her.

Her head pounded. She subdued the throbbing in her brain by mentally running through a checklist of what she knew to be real.

Her tongue poked the raw and empty space in her gums where her teeth used to be. It still hurt, and the pain was real. So was the ache in her legs, and the itch of insect bites on her arms. All real.

So was her need to find Haley.

She left the tree and looked down the way where Jeremiah had gone. He wasn't there anymore, nor was his trail of steam.

She trotted westward. Instinct guided her, and her drive pushed her forward. None of this looked familiar, none of this made sense, but perhaps by some bizarre logic, she felt she would have a better chance of finding Haley if she put as much distance between herself and Jeremiah as possible.

Her eyelids grew heavy, and the temptation of sleep came upon her like a shadow, slipping over her. The pulsing in her head became a metronome, providing a steady beat that rocked her closer to sleep. Before today, she would nap a couple of times a day. The doctor told her that was to be expected, as cancer takes a lot out of a person.

Takes the life out of them...

Twice she lost her balance. Her feet slipped and she grabbed the bare branches to keep from falling. She focused on the rage toward the monsters that boiled inside her.

Briars and thorns poked at her ankles, drawing blood.

She ignored everything her body tried to tell her and continued on, forging her own path through the woods. She needed to stay awake, keep her senses keen, watch and listen for any sound that might lead to Haley.

Her feet tangled in a nest of briars. She went down to one knee, pushing her arms straight out to prevent from face-diving into the mess. The thorns scraped the flesh of her fingers raw, but she swallowed her yelps and waited for the pain to go away, listening to the night.

A sound.

Her eyes shifted in sudden spasms of paranoia as she gazed around her, looking for the source of the sound. Wet slaps.

After a moment, she grabbed the trunk of the nearest tree and began to haul herself back up. She looked out into the forest and closed her eyes, willing the sound to come again.

It did. She opened her eyes and walked out of the briars carefully, yet quickly.

Up ahead there was movement in the trees. Or maybe it was simply a trick of the darkness. Either way, Jane went toward them. She tried to fight against the hope that rose within her, afraid to let herself believe this horrible journey might be nearing its end.

The air grew colder, and the musky stench of rotting wood hung over it all. Skeletal limbs reached out and pricked at her face and her arms. She pushed on, cupping her hands over her eyes to shield them.

Then there was light. A little beam close to the ground gave what small illumination it could to the dense forest. It spun around, shining its light randomly on the circle of trees around it before finally settling, pointing it's light east.

Jane crept forward. A police-issue Maglite, identical to the one Jane owned.

She grabbed the flashlight, feeling its weight, and pointed the beam in front of her.

She stood in a small hollow. Here, the trees grew away from each other. They bordered the hollow, almost like a wall.

More slapping sounds.

She moved the flashlight, waited for her eyes to adjust, and stared in disbelief.

In the gloom of the forest, even with the flashlight, they were almost invisible. But they were there.

She stood in the center of a massacre.

A bone yard of monsters.

Monsters Jane had never seen before. They lay on the ground, eyes open, and blood dripping from their necks or spilling from their gaping mouths. Expressionless, but their features were horrifying.

The rhythm in her head picked up, and the blood drained from her face and tears welled up in her eyes.

She tried to focus on the details of the creatures, but found that she couldn't, for these monsters weren't like the ones Jane had seen. They looked pale as Jane did, and they wore clothing similar to that of police uniforms.

She shook her head and rubbed the tears from her eyes.

You're sick, Jane. Your brain is trying to make you see things that aren't there.

The more she stared at the bodies, the more she became convinced they were not now, nor had they ever been, monsters.

Instead they were the corpses of her once fellow officers, probably part of the search team that had been looking for Haley.

She shined the light over each individual officer, five bodies in total, and did not recognize a single one of them.

More wet slaps.

Jane swung the flashlight beam in the direction of the sounds.

Isaiah sat on the forest floor with its back toward Jane. The monster was hunched over the body of a police officer.

"You," Jane said. Her voice trembled with a fusion of fear and anger.

The monster opened its maw, pulling its long teeth away from the officer's neck. It turned its head, eyes catching like fire in the beam of her flashlight.

Its teeth were stained with a fresh coat of glistening blood.

It let the officer drop to the ground and slowly, Isaiah stood. It stalked over to Jane.

Jane kept the flashlight focused on it as it drew closer. Her lungs pulled in a long, quavering gasp and held it. Jane wanted to back away, but couldn't. She stood there, stiff with terror, and gaped at the deep, black, bottomless pools of eyes looking back at her.

Its hot breath passed by Jane's face in sour little puffs.

Jane reached halfway to the waistband of her jeans, judging Isaiah. There was no reaction. It didn't snarl or lunge for her. It simply watched.

Slowly, inch by trembling inch, she reached the rest of the way and grabbed her gun. She clicked the safety off with her thumb and aimed at the monster. She couldn't stop her hand from quaking, and Isaiah noticed. From behind its cage of teeth, the monster's lips stretched into a smile.

"What did you do with Haley?" Jane said.

At the mention of her niece, Isaiah stiffened.

If Jane's fear had abated even slightly, it had now returned.

She held her ground. This was her monster.

"Isaiah, I'm going to ask you again. Where the fuck is my niece?"

The look on its face, the piercing stare of its eyes, and how every muscle in its body bulged, remaining taut, sent a deep shiver through Jane.

Coldness crept its way through her head, gripping her brain

with long icy fingers. This bud of a headache seemed different than anything else she'd ever felt.

"Isaiah!" she screamed. The monster's eyes brightened. "Where is my—"

A noise cut her off, providing her with the answer she'd been searching for.

In the trees behind Isaiah, the ones that bordered the hollow, a little girl's mournful whimper broke through the night.

Jane cast the flashlight's beam on the space in between the trunks. She saw the purple ribbon on her head before she saw the girl. Haley poked her head out from behind the trees. Her eyes were glazed over, as if she'd been aroused from sleep.

Jane threw a hand over her mouth to stop herself from crying.

She's alive! I knew she'd be alive!

The girl staggered into the hollow, still whimpering. Her clothes were caked with mud and filth.

She had on the same T-shirt she'd worn to school, but her jeans were torn and barely clinging to her body.

And there was blood between her legs. A lot of blood.

CHAPTER 11

A simple conclusion of insanity was pretty tempting right now. It would be so much easier. It would explain everything, and she could dismiss this all like one of her nightmares.

But Haley continued walking toward her, crying, scared.

Isaiah stepped to the side, clearing the path for Jane. The monster still grinned as she passed it. A low clicking noise resonated deep within its chest.

Haley's eyes focused on Jane. At first, a quizzical expression surfaced in her gaze, as if she didn't recognize her aunt. Then her eyes brightened and the corners of her mouth turned up slightly, sweetly.

Jane tucked her gun away, walked a few steps closer, dropped the flashlight and fell to her knees. She opened her arms and took Haley into her embrace. She kissed her forehead and her cheeks and held her tighter.

Haley squeezed too, pushing her face into Jane's chest and sobbing. Jane cried as well, clutching Haley, thinking if she let go, she might lose her all over again.

Jane sensed Isaiah creeping up behind her.

"Haley," Jane said, wiping the tears from her eyes, "can you see them too?"

"Who?"

"The monsters."

"No."

Jane leaned away from her niece and turned, looking at Isaiah. It loomed over her, shoulders hunched, ready to pounce.

"Who took you here?" she asked her. "Who brought you all the way out here?"

A fresh batch of tears washed over Haley. She dug her face

in the nook of Jane's shoulder in the way nervous children do.

"I was scared," she said, her voice muffled in Jane's shirt. "Uncle Dan was hurting me again."

Jane pulled Haley away from her, forcing her to look her in the eyes.

"How was he hurting you?"

"The little games he makes me play. And he hurts me." Haley's eyes flashed downward. Jane followed her gaze to her bloodied groin.

So the pictures were real.

She embraced Haley again.

"I'm sorry, sweetie. I'm so sorry."

"And then you hurt him."

"What?"

"You hurt him. I was scared. I hid in the closet. When I heard you coming back down... I'm sorry I ran away."

Jane rubbed her back. "Sweetie, I didn't hurt you uncle. I loved him. I didn't know about this. If I had known—" Jane trailed off.

Haley broke the hug and stepped backward, chewing on a lock of her hair.

Isaiah towered over them, snarling. Its mouth opened slowly.

"Come on," Jane said, "let's get you home. We'll get you cleaned up and we can explain to the police what happened. Everything will be okay, sweetie."

Jane picked up the flashlight. Haley started to walk past her, shaking her head. She tried to pull away in protest, but was about to trip over the body of the police officer Isaiah had been snacking on.

Jane pulled Haley's wrist and yanked her back, sending the girl into a spin. The girl landed on her butt, clutching her wrist.

Isaiah jumped in front of Jane, crouched low, arms spread wide. Its mouth had fully opened and it dripped with saliva and blood.

Slowly, Jane picked up the flashlight, shining it on Isaiah. Its pupils shrunk in the light. Then she moved the light lower to its feet, where the officer lay... but the officer was no longer there.

She scanned the light around the hollow. The ground was

full of lush, soft green blades of glass. No bodies. No blood.

No evidence the officers had even been there at all, save for the Maglite in Jane's hand. The same kind of Maglite she owned.

Isaiah could have gobbled them up. Or it could have moved the bodies when I wasn't looking. But they were here.

"C'mon," Jane said, "enough is enough."

She picked up Haley again by her wrist. The girl yelped in pain. Jane heard her cry, but it sounded distant; she couldn't take her eyes off of Isaiah.

She'd never seen it this ferocious before. Its eyes boiled like hot tar.

Of course, it doesn't want me to take Haley—its next meal.

The girl doesn't see it, but that doesn't mean the monster isn't there.

It didn't matter what she had to do, as long as she made it out of here with Haley, still safe.

When she made it back to her house, she would drop the gun and face the music. Explain that Grimes tried to confront her in the woods, and what had happened was nothing more than self-defense. They'd have to believe her, wouldn't they? Once they saw the teeth he kicked in, they would realize she couldn't do that to herself.

If they didn't believe her, she'd go to jail. Not like it mattered. She didn't have much time to live anyway, so how long could they really put her in jail?

Haley couldn't be protected from behind bars, and would most likely be sent to live with a foster family.

Jane couldn't let that happen. Not yet. The girl needed to be protected.

So lost within her thoughts, Jane hadn't heard Haley's screams of protest as she pulled the girl away.

"I don't want to go back with you!" she screamed.

The sound jolted Jane into reality. "What?"

"I said I don't want to leave! I'm scared!" She squealed and cried.

A powerful, monstrous arm slammed against Jane's, breaking the bond of aunt and niece.

Jane hit the ground, grabbing her arm, feeling the wet

spread of blood gush between her fingers. It felt numb, and then she tried to move it, numbness blossomed into pain. The pain traveled through her system, like acid injected into her bloodstream.

It touched me.

She opened her mouth and a rush of air and spittle emerged.

Haley's voice called from afar, crying out before dashing behind the safety of the trees.

Jane convulsed on the forest floor. Her body seized and she couldn't stop it. Even in the darkness, Jane saw a blinding white glow behind her eyes. She jittered and jerked and drooled as her brain tried to jumpstart itself.

Then there was stillness and silence for a time as the light within her eyes faded and the darkness once again took over.

She opened her eyes and sat up. Her head felt cold, colder now than it had before.

She picked up the light and looked around the hollow, turning in a wide circle. No Haley. No Isaiah.

"Haley," she called weakly, rising to her feet. "I'm all better now. I promise. C'mon, we need to go."

The gun lay on the grass where she fell. She picked it up. It seemed heavier than only a moment ago.

"Haley!" Jane spun around the hollow, her sense of direction gone.

The monster has to be real now, because it touched me! It left a mark! That's proof I'm not insane.

"HALEY!" Jane screamed and the night echo screamed back at her.

Then came the stench. It wafted in on the night breeze, subtle at first. Jane's eyes watered and her nostrils burned. She covered her nose and mouth with the collar of her shirt.

From behind the trees, a massive figure started to roll up—a nasty, furry thing, covered in blood and filth. It moved silently in the moonlight.

Isaiah.

Jane aimed the gun and squeezed the trigger twice.

The gun kicked back harder than before, almost slapping her in the face.

The creature dropped, and the swirling gun smoke temporarily obscured Jane's vision.

She ran over to the monster, her finger on the trigger, ready to fire the gun into the corpse of the thing haunting her for so long. She shined the light on the body.

Isaiah wasn't there anymore.

Just Haley.

She lay on the ground, on a bed of dead leaves. She'd been shot in the cheek and in the heart.

The muscles in her face were taut, as if still in pain and frozen in the moment when she tried her hardest to cry out.

Behind her there was another cry. Jane whipped around to see Isaiah lumbering toward them, whimpering, tears streaming down its face.

It looked at Jane with sad eyes and then to Haley. It fell on its knees and sobbed with everything it had.

There was tightness in her head. She ran her fingers through her hair, trying to massage away the pain. She saw her brain as a red mass gripped by a monstrous fist, the blood and juice slowly being squeezed from it.

Across the hollow, more figures advanced her way. She pointed the light on them.

Jeremiah and Enoch.

Enoch wobbled and faltered, still unsure of his legs. Jeremiah floated to the right of him, but no steam came from his mouth. Both crying. The three of them connected, forming a semi-circle around Jane and Haley.

Jane dropped to her knees, the pain in her head now reaching its apex. Her breathing quickened, yet each breath turned shallower.

She picked up Haley and held her close, whispering to her. Rocking her to sleep the way she used to whenever she woke from a terrible nightmare.

"I'm sorry," Jane kissed her niece's forehead.

The tears began to flow, burning down her cheeks.

"I'm sorry," this time apologizing to the ghost of her sister.

"I'm sorry," she said once more, now directed to the monsters that surrounded her—the ones that tried to help.

She cradled Haley close.

"I love you, Haley. I love you so much."

The sun waited below the horizon, as if afraid to rise.

She closed her eyes and thought about the cancer. It had finally won. The tumor turned her into something she'd promised herself she'd never become.

A monster.

And there's supposed to be no such thing as monsters.

Jane slid the gun into her mouth like she'd done a hundred times before. She'd developed a taste for gunmetal.

About the Author

Trevor Firetog is an author and filmmaker from Long Island. He has written short stories, novellas, comic books, and film scripts. When he's not reading on the beaches of LI or scavenging used bookstores, he's usually holed up in his office working on a variety of projects. Find him on Facebook, or on Twitter @ TrevorFiretog

Curious about other Crossroad Press books?
Stop by our site:
http://store.crossroadpress.com
We offer quality writing
in digital, audio, and print formats.

Enter the code FIRSTBOOK
to get 20% off your first order from our store!
Stop by today!